Richard Scarry
Cars and Trucks and Things That Go

fuel oil tanker

Have a nice trip!

MISTRESS MOUSE REPAIRS

tow-truck

garage

FUEL

Collins

An imprint of HarperCollins*Publishers*

Ma and Pa and Pickles and
Penny Pig are going on a
picnic.
Here comes Ma with the
picnic basket.
Please hurry up, Ma

SADIE'S ICE CREAM PARLOUR

TOYS

SODY-POP

soft-drink truck

The Pigs are going to the beach to have their picnic. But first, Pa has some shopping to do. He is going to order some things to be delivered to their home. I wonder what those things could be?

station wagon

vintage sportscar

SAM'S SHOE SHOP

shoe delivery car

meter maid

shopping trolley

taxi

pharmacy delivery car

ABC GLASS COMPANY

bookstore delivery van

glass-window truck

TAXI STAND

veteran car

motorbikes

baby pram

STOP

Officer Flossy and her bicycle

Did you see that? Dingo Dog has knocked down almost all the parking meters. What a terrible driver! I think Officer Flossy is going to give him a ticket. At least, she is going to try. We'll see if she succeeds.

a frightened parking meter

a terrible driver

hay wagon

sailing dinghy

statue

delivery truck

MICHAEL ANGELO SCULPTOR

STOP

HAY

SOAPY SUDS WINDOW CLEANER

window cleaner

pickle truck

veteran sportscar

milk van

MILK

PETE'S PICKLES

Dingo drives off before Officer Flossy can give him a ticket. Oh, that Dingo is so naughty! Go get him, Officer Flossy.

dragster

Pa Pig drives past a truck carrying a statue. "Did you see who is in the back with the statue?" Penny asks Pickles. "Yes," says Pickles. "It's Goldbug. He shows up almost everywhere."

alligator car

steam locomotive

guard's van

flatbed trailer

MOLASSES

tanker

tilt-cab truck

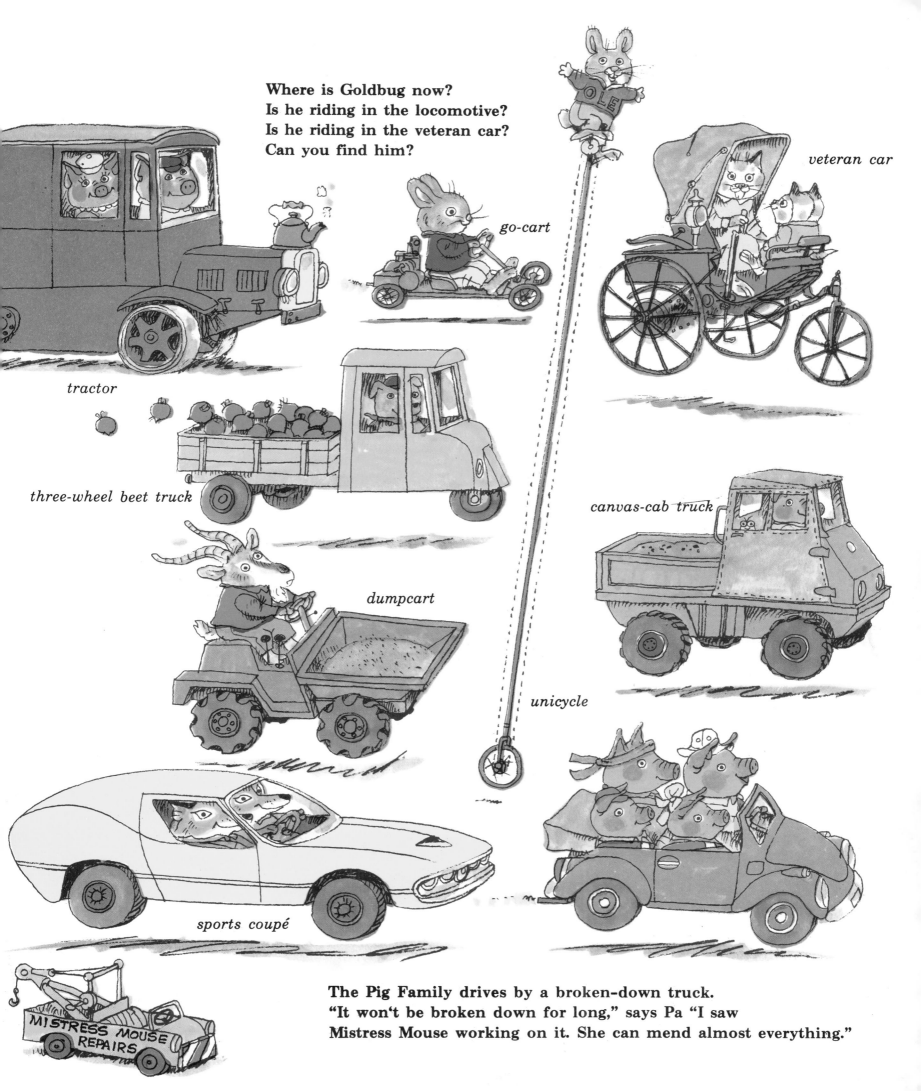

Where is Goldbug now?
Is he riding in the locomotive?
Is he riding in the veteran car?
Can you find him?

veteran car

go-cart

tractor

three-wheel beet truck

canvas-cab truck

dumpcart

unicycle

sports coupé

MISTRESS MOUSE REPAIRS

The Pig Family drives by a broken-down truck.
"It won't be broken down for long," says Pa "I saw
Mistress Mouse working on it. She can mend almost everything."

Faster, Flossy, faster!
Go get Dingo!
But where is that rascal?
Can you see him?

JAKE THE PLUMBER

double-cab pick-up

mouse van

pumpkin car

tractor

mobile crane

Homer drove his tractor into the pond.
That wasn't a very smart thing to do, Homer.

bus

wooden station wagon

pig van

Look! There is Mistress Mouse again. And this time
she is towing a BREAKDOWN TRUCK!
Hello there, Goldbug . . . wherever you are!

a wrecked car being towed by a BIG BREAKDOWN TRUCK
which is being towed by a little breakdown truck

MISTRESS MOUSE
REPAIRS

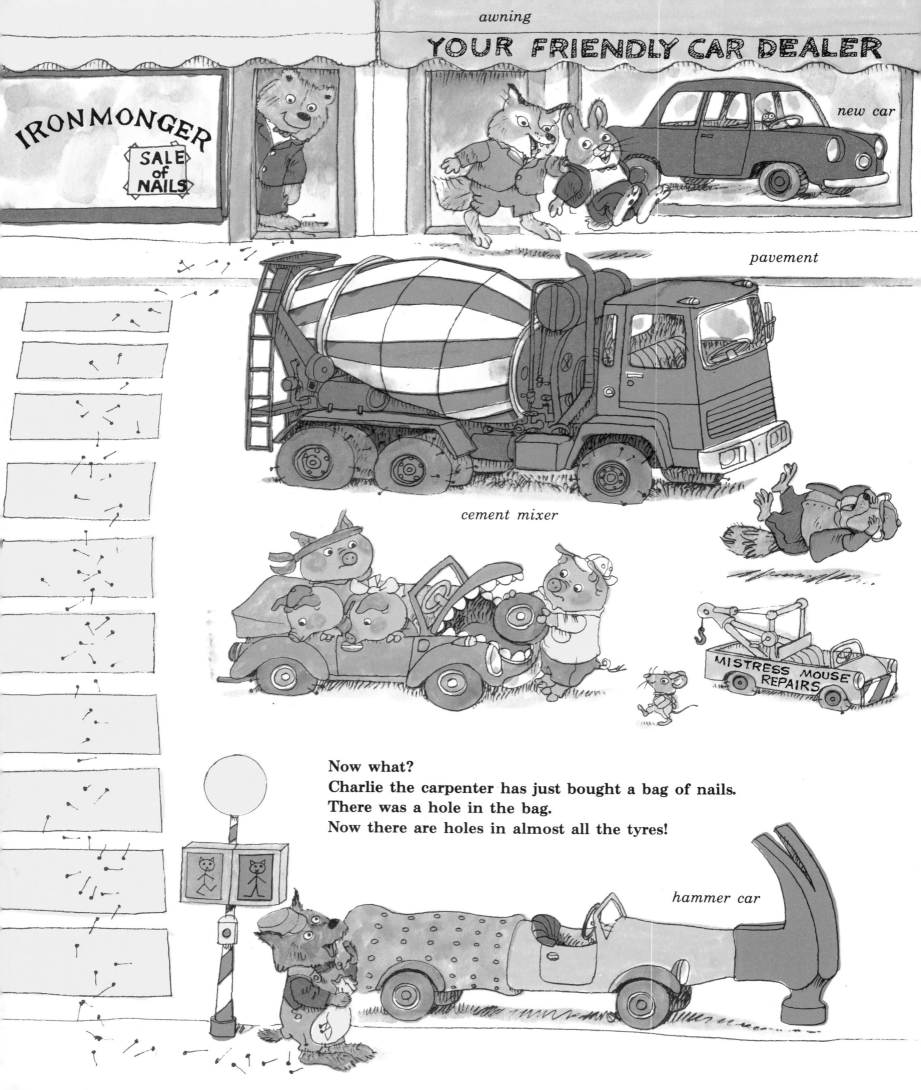

IRONMONGER

SALE of NAILS

awning

YOUR FRIENDLY CAR DEALER

new car

pavement

cement mixer

MISTRESS MOUSE REPAIRS

Now what?
Charlie the carpenter has just bought a bag of nails.
There was a hole in the bag.
Now there are holes in almost all the tyres!

hammer car

USED CARS

used car

school bus

SCHOOL BUS

hard hat

flat tyre

veteran open car

Where's Dingo? How did he manage not to get a flat tyre? I see Officer Flossy is riding on the pavement.
Keep after him, Flossy!
Hello, Goldbug . . . wherever you are.

elevated tower truck

STOP

trolley bus

bug bus

motor scooter

SIGHTSEEING TOURS

sightseeing bus

yellow
violet
orange
brown
red
blue
green
pink

PAUL THE PAINTER

a painter's pick-up truck

LIBRARY

drain cleaner

ditch-digger

mobile crane

SQUEEZE LEFT
ROAD CONSTRUCTION
AHEAD

ant bus

hot-dog car

rumble-seat sportscar

coupé with open back hatch

Pa is worn out from changing the
tyre. He is taking a nap in the back seat
while Ma drives.
All right, everyone! Slow down! There is
road construction ahead.

coupé with open sun-roof

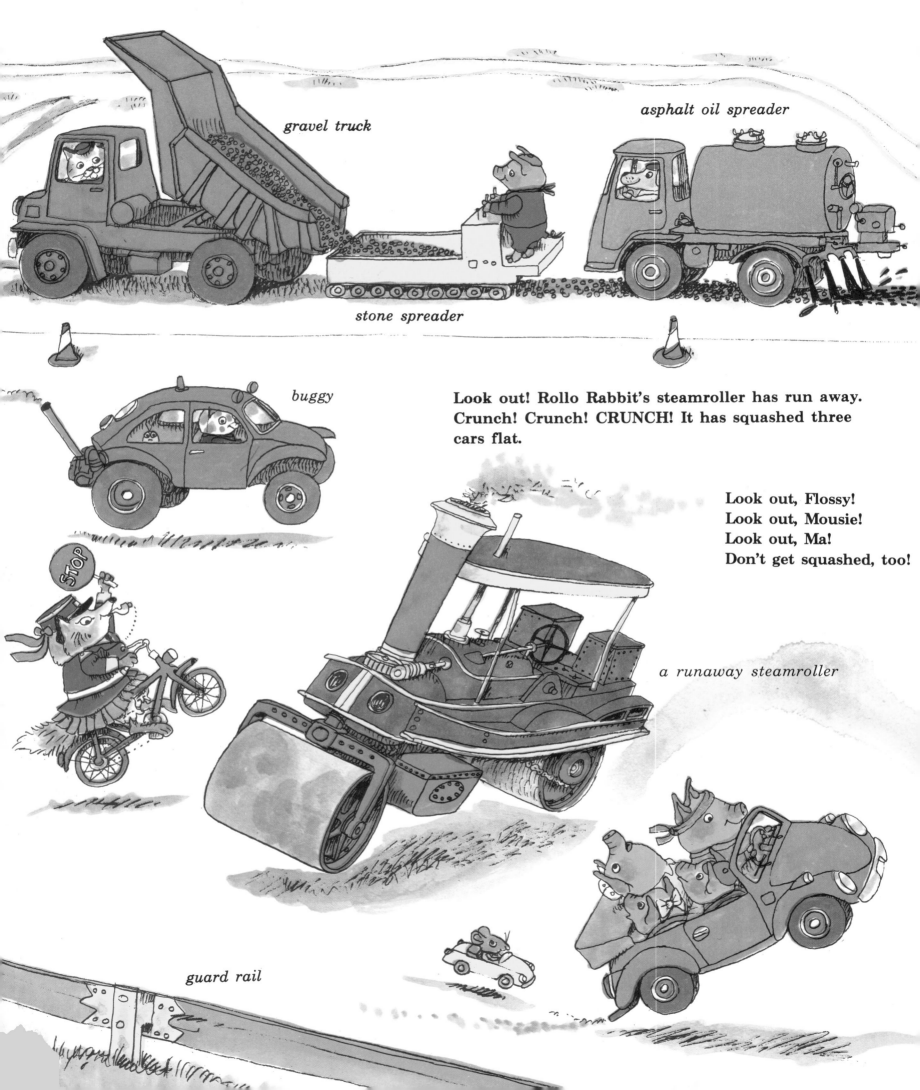

gravel truck

asphalt oil spreader

stone spreader

buggy

Look out! Rollo Rabbit's steamroller has run away.
Crunch! Crunch! CRUNCH! It has squashed three
cars flat.

Look out, Flossy!
Look out, Mousie!
Look out, Ma!
Don't get squashed, too!

a runaway steamroller

STOP

guard rail

roller

The workers are finishing the new road.
The last thing they have to do is paint the dividing lines.

road
stripers

KEEP
LEFT

motor caravan

FRESH
EGGS

egg truck

airport limousine

AIRPORT LIMOUSINE

motorcycle

motor scooter

tandem

Maniacbug

Goodness! Who is that making a mess of the line? That's not Goldbug, is it?
No, it can't be Goldbug. He would never do a thing like that. That fellow must be Maniacbug.

sports coupé

bookshelf-maker's car

Keep left, everyone. Drive slowly on to the new road.

farm tractor

a tired traveller

hay-and-pig wagon (Make a wish!)

mini-bus

veteran car

STOP

IN

toothbrush car

petrol tanker

PETROL

petrol pump

hose

car washer

REST ROOMS

a woodchuck
in a hurry

CAR WASH

mini-jeep

canopied vintage car

toothpaste car

EXIT

oil cans

attendant

Ma Pig sees that they are running low on petrol, so she drives into the petrol station to fill up the tank. I can find Goldbug, but I can't see the Pig Family. Where do you suppose they have gone?

lift

dirty station wagon

car greaser

hook-and-ladder truck

rescue truck

ALL RIGHT!
Who left the water
running in that
fire engine?

water tower truck

fire alarm box

siren

hose

Fire Master's car

CHIEF

The Pig Family is refreshed. The petrol tank is full again, and Pa is back at the wheel.

nozzle

ambulance

Ladybug has a fire in her car and the firemen have come to put it out.
Can you guess who called them?

helmet

bell

pumping truck

fire point

diesel locomotive

mail wagon

tanker wagon

goods wagon

forklift

All the wheels need to be
oiled so they won't squea.
Squeaky Mouse says so.

Tom Turtle's car

veteran car

gardener's truck

car wagon

double-decker coach

steam locomotive

railway station

CLOVER

station wagon

doughnut car

DOUGHNUTS

Railway stations are busy places. There are always lots of people coming and going. Goods trains load and unload letters, food, parcels and all sorts of things.

"I am hungry," says Pickles.
"I am too," says Pa,
"Now just be patient," says Ma. "It won't be long before we have our picnic. But first we must stop at Grandma Pig's farm and buy some fresh corn."

STOP

corn picker

hay gatherer

At Grandma Pig's farm, all the farmhands are very busy.
They are picking corn, gathering hay and delivering milk.
They are harvesting wheat which will be made into bread.
Grandpa is cutting the grass and Grandma is clanking
around on her old steam tractor.
My! what a busy farm!

milk cans

corn car

Auntie Pastry and Cousin Willie are selling fresh corn.
It looks so good, Pa just has to take a bite.
"No, Pa," says Ma. "Don't eat it yet! Wait until I cook it!"

well

FRESH CORN

grain harvester

wheat

tractor

Grandma's steam tractor

grass cutter

Wolfwagon

swimming
tank

swimming jeep

landing craft

desert jeep

motorcycle
and sidecar

tractor motorcycle

General Nuisance's car

water jeep

jeep

half-track
troop carrier

bridge

Won't you please wake up, Mister Soldier?

tent

The Pigs have bought their corn and are on their way to the beach for their picnic. They are passing an army camp. Look at all the soldiers!

chapel truck

canteen truck

radio truck

old-style tank

ambulance

old armoured car

tank

army car

gun tractor

civilian car

Look at all the soldiers!
These soldiers are going home for the weekend to
visit their families. Their car is just like an army
car, but it is painted differently.

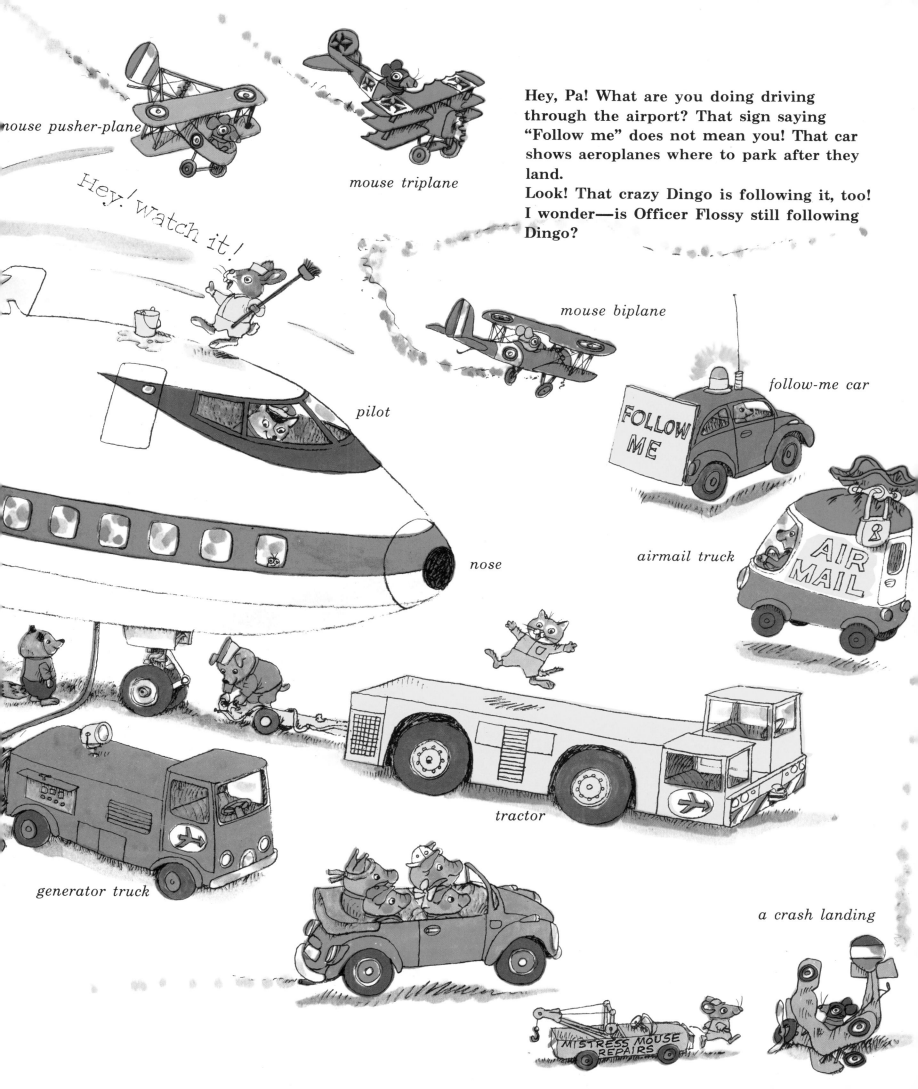

mouse pusher-plane

mouse triplane

Hey! Watch it!

Hey, Pa! What are you doing driving through the airport? That sign saying "Follow me" does not mean you! That car shows aeroplanes where to park after they land.
Look! That crazy Dingo is following it, too! I wonder—is Officer Flossy still following Dingo?

mouse biplane

pilot

follow-me car

FOLLOW ME

AIR MAIL

airmail truck

nose

tractor

generator truck

a crash landing

MISTRESS MOUSE REPAIRS

shark car

ICE CREAM

ice-cream truck

sand dune

mouse beach buggy

sand yacht

Oh, Piggy, you made a mistake!
Your car won't run in the water.
Only a propeller car can do that.

propeller car

fringe car

BATH HOUSE

shower

refreshment stand

beach buggies

roll bars protect
the driver in case
the buggy rolls over

"AT LAST!" says Ma. "We are at the
beach and we are going to have a nice
quiet picnic. Pa, maybe you should put
a shirt on. I think you are getting
sunburned."
"Oh, I'll be all right," says Pa.

go-anywhere buggy

pedal boat

submarine

forklift

The picnic is over, and Pa is not all right.
He is all RED! WOW! What a sunburn!
Pa is also all stuffed, with food. A nap is
just what he needs, so Ma drives for a while.
Close your mouth when you sleep, Pa!

dock propeller

tugboat

air-cushion ferry (hovercraft)

FERRY

FERRY

TICKET OFFICE

crane

flag

radar

smokestack

lifeboat

a furious captain

anchor

cargo freighter

a falling car

tender car

barge

Pa is missing all the sights of the harbour. Cars are being loaded on to a freighter, to be carried across the ocean to far parts of the world.
Oh, my! One of them is not going any farther than the bottom of the harbour!

straddle truck

flying fish

FISH

fish truck

dustcart

WATCH WHAT YOU'RE DOING!!

squasher-downer

bulldozer

a squashed-down golf cart

Two golfers have lost their golf balls in the rubbish dump. Please help find them.

TOWN DUMP

caterpillar bus

cross-country car

The Pig Family is driving up into the mountains. It is getting colder. It is snowing. The road is icy. The pie truck skids off the road.

Mistress Mouse says it is time to put on snow chains. Hey Pa! Wake up! Put on your snow chains! And please put the top up.

a skidding pie truck

SLIPPERY WHEN WET

icy road

bent sign

MISTRESS MOUSE REPAIRS

MOM'S PIES

a worker stringing wire on telephone poles

TELEPHONE COMPANY

spool of wire

telephone truck

snow bus

Ma put on the snow chains.
Ma put the top up.
WOW! Just look at all that snow! Isn't it beautiful?
There's a pile of things all covered with snow on the truck
behind the Pigs. I wonder what they could be?

Harry dear!
You must remember
to close the
window
after you!

snowplough

sledge

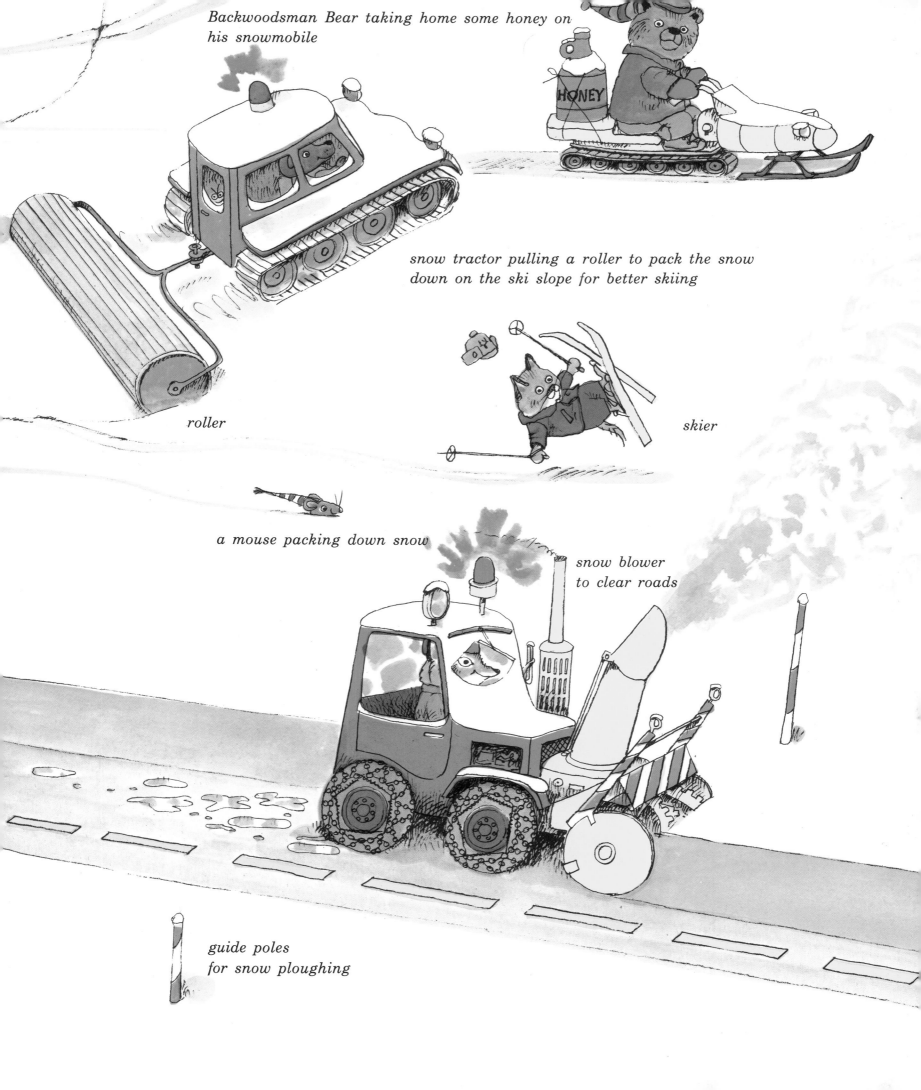

Backwoodsman Bear taking home some honey on his snowmobile

HONEY

snow tractor pulling a roller to pack the snow down on the ski slope for better skiing

roller

skier

a mouse packing down snow

snow blower to clear roads

guide poles for snow ploughing

express truck
and trailers

EXPRESS 1

tipped-over
watermelon truck

STOP!

Did you guess what those things were, all covered
with snow?
Well! Now you KNOW! They are watermelons.
STOP, WATERMELONS, STOP!

Henry, chasing a watermelon

vintage car

cement mixer

The noise of the rolling watermelons wakens Pa.
Ma stops and Pa takes off the snow chains.
They have come down out of the mountains, and
there is no more snow.
Now Ma is helping Pa put the top down, as the
snow is all melted . . . well, almost all melted.

snow chains

runaway watermelons

EXPRESS 2

EXPRESS 3

STOP

chemical
tanker

mountain
climber

Harry, chasing
a watermelon

STOP!

Carl Cat's car

sportscar

skis on a rack

snowshoe

SKI SCHOOL

ski-school bus

Oh, NO!
I never thought I would see an accident
as bad as this one! This is what I would
call SOME ACCIDENT!
It just doesn't seem possible, does it?
But there you are . . . you can see
for yourself.
And poor Mistress Mouse! It will
probably take her a MILLION YEARS
to mend everything.
Luckily, no one was badly hurt.

STOP

WHIPPED CREAM

FIRE DE

FLOUR

TOMATO JUICE

BANANAS

FRESH EGGS

MISTRESS MOUSE REPAIRS

The egg men always wear seat belts so that they
won't fall out and get broken. Do you?

"Well, we are almost home now," says Pa. "Thank goodness," says Ma.

And, sure enough, here they are.
"BACK, SAFE, HOME AGAIN," they all say together.
In front of their house, a delivery man is just leaving.
"What are those boxes on the front lawn?" asks Ma.
"What are those boxes on the front lawn?" asks Penny.
"What are those boxes on the front lawn?" asks Pickles.
Pa just smiles and doesn't ask anything.
"Oh, look!" says Ma. "I think we are going to have new neighbours."
"Oh, goody," say Penny and Pickles.

delivery van

advertising car

mobile library

EDDIE AND SON — ELECTRICIANS

electrician's van

Take care, Mr Loving

THE 3 MOVERS

TENDER, LOVING, AND CARE

moving van

ADAM'S APPLES

apple van

battery-powered car

WE PRESS SUITS WHILE U WAIT

You missed a wrinkle, Joe!

steamroller

Have you read these other books about the busy world of Richard Scarry?

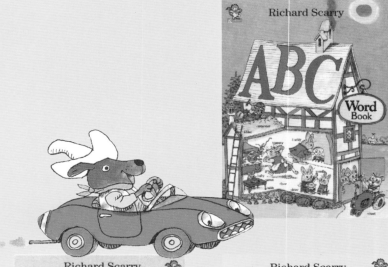

Richard Scarry
ABC Word Book

Richard Scarry
Cars and Trucks and Things That Go

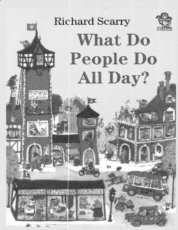

Richard Scarry
What Do People Do All Day?

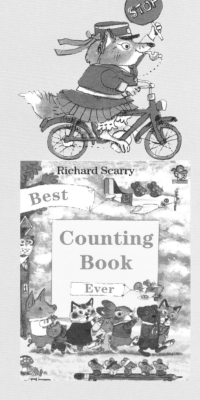

Richard Scarry
Best
Counting Book
Ever

Richard Scarry
Busiest People Ever

Richard Scarry
Funniest Storybook Ever